Story by Miriam Cohen • Picture~~~~~~~~~~~~~~~ban

BEST FRIENDS

MACMILLAN PUBLISHING CO., INC.

New York

COLLIER MACMILLAN PUBLISHERS

London

Macmillan Publishing Co., Inc.
866 Third Avenue, New York, N.Y. 10022
Collier Macmillan Canada Ltd. ISBN 0-02-722800-2
Library of Congress catalog card number: 70-146620
Printed in the United States of America

10   9   8   7   6

The pictures are three-color preseparated pen-and-wash
drawings. The text is set in Helvetica.

For Vivian and George

Jim was waiting outside of school.

He was waiting to say "Hi" to Paul.

Paul was his best friend.

Jim was almost sure of it.

But Paul was late. He came just when the bell rang.
Everybody began running into school.

Jim ran too. He was calling, "Hi, Paul!"
But he tripped. When he got up, Paul was already inside.

Everybody ran to look at the eggs in the incubator.

A light was keeping the eggs warm. When it was time, baby chicks would come out.

"I can't just keep on waiting!" said Danny.
"These eggs are taking too long!"

He yelled, "Come on, Paul. Let's build blocks."

Jim began to make a picture of himself.
He looked in a mirror. Then he drew what he saw.

But the boy in the mirror and the boy
he was drawing did not look the same.

Willy shouted at Sammy, "If you don't
give me that hat, I won't be your best friend."

Margaret painted two girls stuck together.
"They're best friends," she said.

Paul was dragging a long block. Jim was going
to help him, but Anna-Maria got in his way.
"Who's your best friend, Jim?" she asked.

Before Jim could answer, Willy shouted,
"All right, Sammy. I'm not your best friend any more.
I'm Jim's best friend. Right, Jim?"

And Anna-Maria said, "I could be your best friend, Jim.
I could tell you all the things you're supposed to do in school."

Jim didn't know what he should say.
Willy was his friend, but not his best friend.
And Anna-Maria was a girl!

Just then the teacher brought the juice and cookies.
Jim and Paul always sat together.

But Paul said, "So!
Everybody is your best friend except me!"

Paul wouldn't sit near Jim.

Jim couldn't explain what had happened.
And the cookies were the plain kind.

After snack was playground.
Everybody rushed out.

"Oh dear!" the teacher said,
"I didn't bring the balls.
    Paul and Jim, would you get them?"

The classroom was very quiet.

Paul and Jim got the balls out of the cupboard.

They didn't look at each other.

Suddenly Jim shouted, "Paul! The light is out!
The baby chicks will die!"

Paul said, "I'll get the janitor!"
Jim cried, "I'll keep the eggs warm!"
He tried to be as warm as he could.

Everybody came running.
Mr. Wilkins put in a new bulb.

Then he touched the eggs gently.
"They're still plenty warm.
They're going to be all right."

Everyone was cheering.

Danny said, "Jim and Paul saved the baby chicks' lives."

"They really did," said the teacher.

Then Jim knew it.
And Paul knew it.
They could feel it.
They could feel they really were best friends.